THE RENDING

A PREQUEL TO THE COST OF KNOWING

THE STONE CYCLE

ALLAN N. PACKER

LUMINANT PUBLICATIONS

The Rending
A Prequel to The Cost of Knowing

Copyright © 2019 by Allan N. Packer

First edition (v1.6) published in 2019
by Luminant Publications

The characters and events portrayed in this book are fictitious. Any similarity to real persons, living or dead, is coincidental and not intended by the author.

ISBN 978-1-925898-19-4

Luminant Publications
PO Box 305
Greenacres, South Australia 5086

http://www.allanpacker.com

Cover Design by Karri Klawiter

Map illustration by Brian Plush

THE RENDING
A PREQUEL TO THE COST OF KNOWING

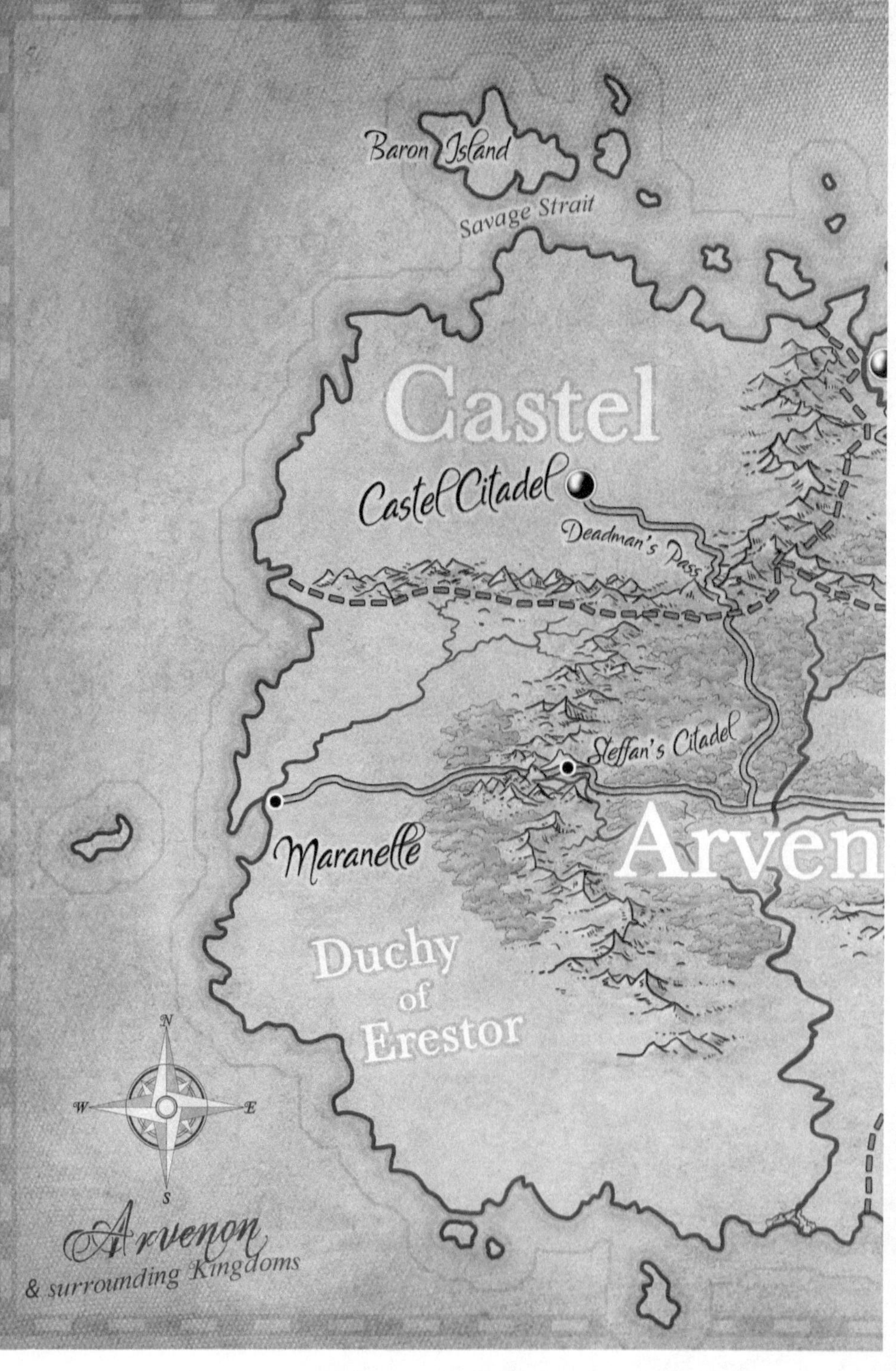

Baron Island
Savage Strait
Castel
Castel Citadel
Deadman's Pass
Steffan's Citadel
Maranelle
Arven
Duchy
of
Erestor
N
W
E
S
Arvenon
& surrounding Kingdoms

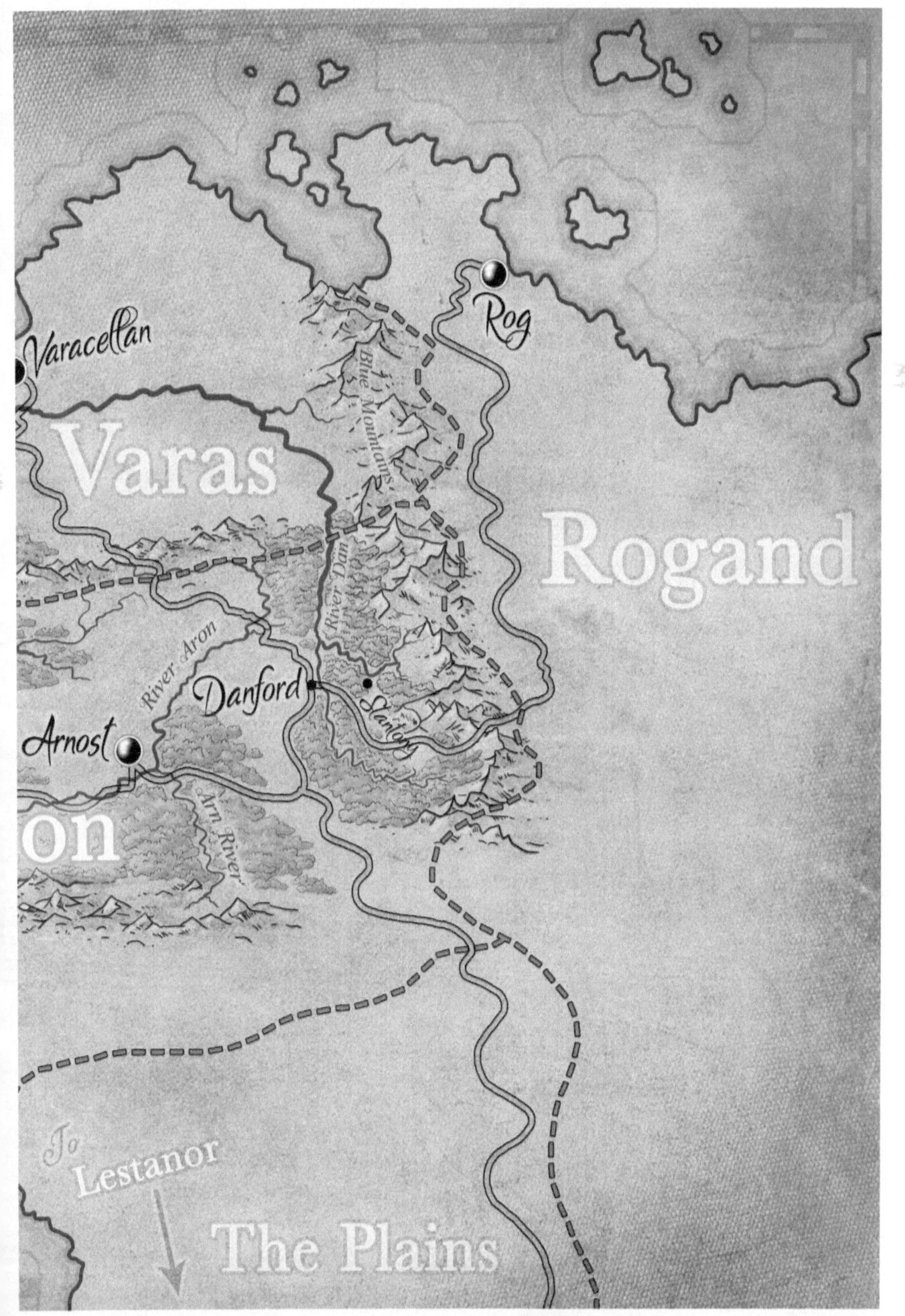

Varacellan
Varas
Rogand
Rog
Blue Mountains
River Dan
River Aron
Danford
Slanton
Arnost
Arn River
on
To Lestanor
The Plains

1

———

The scythes swept back and forth, back and forth, beating time to the slow and rhythmic beat of an ancient dance. Lord Neave watched the progress of the reapers with considerable satisfaction. This year's harvest was beyond encouraging. The yield had been exceptional throughout Erestor, but the Neave ancestral lands to the north with their rich soil and well watered valleys continued to be the envy of the entire region.

The nobleman's reverie was interrupted by the arrival of his seneschal. The elderly retainer coughed delicately before speaking. "The Lord Asturle has arrived and wishes to speak with you, My Lord," he reported, following up his comments with a stiff bow.

The seneschal had been his family's chief steward for longer than Lord Neave could remember. Now an old man, the steward was much too proper to offer comment on members of the nobility, but Lord Neave could read his dour expression well enough to see that he did not approve of the visitor.

"Thank you, Pralven," he said. The seneschal bowed again, before turning on his heel and setting off for the manor house.

Lord Neave sighed deeply. Then he got up and followed the steward.

He arrived to find his wife waiting for him, their two-year-old son in her arms. "I've installed Asturle in the parlor," she told him. "He's in quite a state. I sent one of the servants to offer him a stiff drink," she added, rolling her eyes and shaking her head.

"As always, your good sense is matched by your thoughtfulness, My Lady," he replied with a smile. He paused long enough to plant affectionate kisses on both Lady Neave and his son.

The nobleman headed for the parlor, less than enthusiastic about this latest interaction. He was willing to help, but he wasn't optimistic that his young neighbor would follow through on any advice he might offer. Lord Asturle had come into his inheritance barely six months previously, after the sudden death of his father. In that brief period he had shown himself to be both volatile and impetuous. It was a dangerous combination in a nobleman, especially when combined with the inexperience of youth.

The young lord was pacing the room when his host entered. He turned to Lord Neave anxiously. "Dunnridge claims I have no right to sit on Erestor's Council of Lords. He's threatening to have me thrown out! What can I do?" Tension twisted Asturle's face.

So Lord Dunnridge had been meddling again. Lord Neave had never trusted him. The ambitious nobleman, now in early middle age, had a well established reputation for subtlety. Lord Neave simply thought of him as devious.

Not for the first time, Lord Neave wondered how Dunnridge had managed to establish such a hold over the youth. There must be some dark secret behind it. What didn't he know?

It was clearly time to do some digging—he would ask one of his people to make a few discreet inquiries.

"It's nonsense, Asturle." Lord Neave told him. "Lord Dunnridge is a bully, and it's never wise to yield to bullies. I'll support you, and others on the council will as well. You have to stand your ground, though. With your father gone, it's up to you now."

The conversation centered on the upcoming council meeting, scheduled for three days hence. Much was said, although from Lord Neave's perspective the value of it was questionable. Lord Asturle did, however, leave with the promise of his neighbor's backing should any move be made against him.

Throughout the interaction Lord Neave had freely offered the benefit of his wisdom as always. He entertained little hope that any of his suggestions would be heeded.

Even before the young nobleman was out of sight, Lord Neave called for one of his retainers. "I need you to make some inquiries for me, Billson. Why is Lord Asturle under so much pressure? Has he inherited debts that we don't know about? Have there been indiscretions with the wrong woman?"

Billson bowed, and set off without delay.

Lord Neave sought out his wife. "Something isn't right. I don't understand why Asturle is so anxious. I've sent Billson to see what he can uncover."

"Billson is a good choice. If there's anything to unearth he'll expose it, and he'll do it tactfully. He also knows how to handle himself if something goes wrong."

They wandered outside and stood together enjoying the sight of their son toddling around in the garden among the flowers.

"I find these situations so frustrating," said Lord Neave, shaking his head. "I wish I could get beyond the posturing and find out what's really going on in Asturle's head. Dunnridge's too, for that matter."

"You're the most sensible and down-to-earth person I know, but you're still a dreamer," she told him with a smile. "I love that about you."

He shook his head. "It isn't just a dream—not if my great grandfather could be believed. He lived to a great old age, and he used to tell me stories when I was little. Apparently there was a family tradition about a matriarch with a magical talisman that showed her what people were thinking. It made quite an impression on him—he often talked about it, and he told me he believed it was true. The talisman was probably a fable, but sometimes I still wish I could borrow it."

"What happened to this supposed talisman?" she asked.

He shrugged. "I don't know. He didn't want to talk about that. Apparently it all ended very badly."

Seeing the skeptical look on her face, he changed the subject. "In the morning I'll be leaving early for Maranelle for the council meeting, Anneka," he said. "I expect to be away for several days."

"The harvesting is almost over. You wanted the men to hone their soldiering skills," she reminded him.

"You're right. Their training is overdue. The duke will be on my back if I don't keep our contingent well prepared."

"I could organize a session while you're away."

He looked uncertain for a moment, then he shrugged. "Why not?" he said with a grin. "The men will follow your lead enthusiastically, even though you'll drive them much harder than I ever would! I've seen you in action, and it's a wonder to behold." He wrapped her in a warm embrace. "You're a rare woman, Anneka," he told her proudly. "Not one of the other lords has a wife with any hope of organizing his soldiers effectively."

"I seriously doubt that any of the other lords would want such a wife!" she retorted.

"It's their loss, then," he said with a wink.

"Since you're so impressed with my skills, why don't you put them to the test? Give me half of the men, and I'll challenge you to a mock battle," she dared him with a grin.

"Not a chance!" he protested. "I'd never survive the embarrassment if you won. And you probably would!"

"If you hurry home from the council I might let you in on some of my strategies. There might be other benefits as well," she teased.

He laughed, drawing her close once again.

———

Asturle squirmed as Lord Dunnridge fixed him in a merciless glare.

"Are you going to cooperate?" Dunnridge demanded.

"I can't do it! It wouldn't be right!"

"Notions of right and wrong didn't seem to bother you when you murdered your father."

The young nobleman writhed. "It wasn't like that," he protested.

"What was it like?" Dunnridge mocked. "Are you suggesting your father poisoned himself?"

Asturle shuddered uncontrollably, but could find nothing to say.

"You weren't nearly careful enough, you young fool. You can't rely on other people to do your dirty work. Not unless you arrange an accident for them once they've finished.

"You thought you could buy the silence of your man. All you did was fund his drinking habit and loosen his wagging tongue in the bargain. You should have slipped a knife into him and saved your money. If you could have found the courage!" Dunnridge stared at him with open contempt on his face.

The young nobleman tore his eyes away, unable to meet Dunnridge's gaze.

"Let me make it very simple for you," Dunnridge continued. "You'll do as I say, or tomorrow at the council I will charge you with murder. I have your accomplice under my protection, and he will testify against you. You'll be finished! You won't just lose your place on the council. You'll be tried and executed. Don't expect forgiveness, and don't imagine you'll receive mercy. None of the council members can afford to tolerate behavior like this. Not when they know they might be next."

He paused, clearly enjoying Asturle's discomfort.

"Do as I say," said Dunnridge, "and I will arrange for your accomplice to disappear. Permanently."

A complacent smile came to the tormentor's lips. "You might find that your land holdings increase as well. No one can ever have too much land."

Asturle hung his head, too terrified to respond.

PENNANTS WHIPPED in the breeze as the battle lines swayed back and forward. Clusters of onlookers, mostly children, cheered the men on from the sidelines. The two groups of men fought with wooden swords, but they were not holding back.

Lady Neave watched it all with a keen eye, intent on deciding whether she had chosen her leaders well. She allowed them to continue the struggle for two hours without a break.

The sun was nearing its zenith when the seneschal appeared with refreshments. "My Lady," he said with a bow. He held out a plate containing food and drink.

"Thank you, Pralven," she said, selecting a sweetmeat. "This will do very well."

On impulse she pointed toward the battle. "What do you think of my formations?"

"Very pretty, Your Ladyship," he replied, a dour expression on his face.

She laughed out loud. It wasn't intentional, but the mirth sneaked past her defenses.

The steward didn't react at all. "Will that be all, My Lady?" he asked, austere as ever.

"Yes, Pralven. Thank you."

He bowed again and departed without further ado.

Lady Neave gazed at his retreating back with a wry smile. Crusty as he was, she knew that he liked her. Nevertheless, it was obvious that he didn't approve of what she was doing. And she had no doubt that others shared his views. Organizing soldiers simply wasn't women's work.

Their disapproval didn't deter her, though. The training needed to be done. And as one of the senior nobles in Erestor, her husband had far too many responsibilities as it was.

She was, however, honest enough to admit to herself that lightening her husband's load was not her only motivation. The truth was that she was enjoying herself immensely.

And she knew she was good at it.

She had always been an organizer. There was no denying that growing up as a member of the nobility had offered her opportunities to lead that most children would never experience. She had never traded on her status, though. As a child she had routinely joined in the rough physical games of the common born boys her own age. She had more than held her own against them, and before long she had become their undisputed leader.

Even when her parents noticed her bruises, they hadn't restrained her. They'd given her an unusual amount of latitude in the way she developed and expressed her burgeoning leadership abilities.

Everything had changed when she turned sixteen. Her parents insisted that she emerge from childhood as a young lady, not as a bruised and battered tomboy. The change of focus had been an unwelcome shock at first, but she had eventually embraced it as a challenge.

The transformation had apparently been successful, too, because there'd been no shortage of suitors. She treated all of them with equal disdain. Her attitude hadn't changed until she met Collin, heir to the extensive Neave estate. She quickly discovered that he was her equal both intellectually and organizationally. In spite of their age difference—he was a dozen years older than her—they had fallen madly in love. They were married a few short weeks before Collin's father had died suddenly, catapulting his son and heir into a position of overwhelming responsibility. Thankfully, Collin had been groomed from childhood for the role of a major landholder and influential nobleman.

The newlyweds had worked hard together to establish the new Lord Neave among his peers in Erestor. Like her parents before him, her husband had allowed her considerable freedom to initiate and lead. Her role that day in the combat training would never have been possible if she hadn't already established herself as an authority figure among those beholden to the Neave family.

Even the eventual arrival of their son, Donnie—for some reason he had been a long time coming—hadn't slowed her down. He was the light of her life, but the experience of motherhood hadn't diminished her energy in the slightest.

She closed her eyes for a moment, shutting out the conflict and allowing herself to recall the delight on Donnie's little face that morning as he ran to her, arms open wide.

· · ·

THE SOUNDS of battle drew her back to the present. Opening her eyes, she abandoned her musing and looked around her. The combatants were tiring, so she decided to call for a break. As the men paused, exhausted, she went to speak to the two leaders.

"You're doing well, Hydin," she told one of the men. "You know what's needed. Don't be frightened to insist that your men follow your lead closely."

She turned to the other man. "You have the makings of a fine natural leader, Yosef. So lead! That doesn't mean doing it all yourself. Your role is to point the way, then give others the opportunity to try it for themselves."

Yosef nodded wearily as he leaned on his wooden sword.

She turned to face all of the men. "Take a break for one hour," she called. "Then you can go at it again."

Her words were greeted with a chorus of groans.

"You might not like it now, but you'll thank me if you ever find yourselves doing this for real!" she told them unrepentantly.

With the mock battle on hold, she set off to oversee the archers.

A group of about twenty men had positioned themselves two hundred paces from a line of practice targets. The targets now resembled porcupines. Lady Neave watched closely as the bowmen set about their task. It was quickly obvious that the group included several fine archers.

After watching for a considerable period, she picked out five of the men and spoke to them before calling the whole group together. "I've selected five of your number. I've asked them to stop practicing for a while, and take time instead to give guidance to the rest of you. Make sure you listen to them closely!

"All of you are doing well. Keep at it."

She watched as her select group began observing the others and offering advice on their technique. Satisfied, she left the archers and returned to the main group. She glanced up at the sun. It was time to resume the trial battle.

She kept all of the men working hard until late afternoon. Then she dismissed them.

The exercises had clearly shown her who had leadership abilities or potential, and which of the men were the most capable fighters. She would pass on the information to her husband. He would want to specially groom them to ensure they were properly trained, fully equipped against the day when they might be called upon to defend king and country.

On her way back to the manor house she was intercepted by Father Bryan, the aged rector of the parish church. He appeared to be as calm as ever—she could never remember seeing him perturbed. It was as though his face with its deep wrinkles had been carved from rock. But the light in his eyes seemed strangely dimmed.

"Are you well, Father?" she asked him.

"I am well, My Lady. I thank you," he replied. He paused for a moment, searching her face. "I was praying for Lord Neave this morning," he said. "As I did so my spirit was greatly troubled."

She didn't know what to say.

He took her hand and squeezed it delicately. "Do not put your hope in princes, My Lady. God alone can sustain you."

Then he was gone, leaving her bemused, wondering at the meaning of his words.

Was some kind of trouble brewing at the council? She knew that the meeting would bring a range of challenges for Lord Neave. He always told her in detail what transpired there, so she knew that the meetings were rarely straightforward. On occasion the interactions between some of the noblemen might best be described as a war of words.

Not for the first time, she wished she could be there in person to support him.

2

The council meeting began at the scheduled time. Meetings were usually overseen by the Duke of Erestor, the king's uncle and the highest ranking of the nobles. On this occasion the duke was visiting Arnost, the capital of Arvenon, so in his absence the meeting was chaired by Lord Leile, a senior nobleman held universally in high regard. All of the other local nobles were present, with the exception of Lord Burtelen, who was unable to attend due to ill health.

As soon as the meeting commenced, Lord Dunnridge rose to his feet. "My Lord," he said, with a nod to Lord Leile, "I have an extraordinary piece of business to raise. The nature of it is such that it cannot be delayed."

Lord Leile frowned. "What business is this, Dunnridge?"

"I need to defer to our friend and colleague, Lord Asturle." Dunnridge nodded curtly to the man in question and sat down.

The young nobleman stood slowly to his feet and coughed nervously. He stole a glance at Dunnridge then stared at his feet.

"Well?" prompted Lord Leile impatiently.

"I regret to tell you that I have witnessed one of our number plotting against the king," he stammered. He took a deep breath. "The plotter is Lord Neave."

There was an immediate uproar. Lord Neave frowned and shook his head in bewilderment.

Lord Leile rose to his feet. "Order!" he shouted. He waited until the din died down, then he turned to Lord Asturle. "What nonsense is this?" he demanded.

"It's true, I tell you!" Asturle insisted sullenly.

"All of us know the character of Lord Neave. And all of you are aware that no such charge can be received without at least two witnesses," said Lord Leile. "So produce your second witness, or I'll have you thrown out of the meeting!"

Lord Dunnridge rose to his feet. "I am the second witness," he stated evenly, ignoring the pandemonium that followed his statement.

Lord Neave's eyes narrowed. He was well aware that Asturle was terrified of Dunnridge. He was now beginning to grasp the reason why Dunnridge had wanted the young nobleman firmly in his grip. Surely none of the council members would take this supposed conspiracy seriously, though.

"Lord Neave is not satisfied with his current position of influence," Dunnridge continued. "His plan is to draw other members of this council into a scheme designed to discredit the Duke of Erestor. He told me this himself. Naturally, I refused any involvement in such treasonous behavior."

Lord Neave surged to his feet. "These are vicious lies, as both of you well know," he said, barely able to contain his outrage. He fixed his gaze on Lord Asturle. "I know that Dunnridge has some kind of hold over you, but even so I expected better of you," he said, struggling to keep his voice steady.

Asturle refused to meet his gaze.

"I appeal to the duke, and if necessary, to the king!" Lord Neave declared.

"You will certainly have your opportunity to present your case to the duke," Lord Leile assured him.

"In the meantime," said Dunnridge, "I propose that Lord Neave be arrested and held over for further questioning."

Lord Neave battled to master his fury. "I refuse to listen to this nonsense for another moment," he said. He pushed back his chair and headed for the door.

"He should be restrained!" Dunnridge insisted.

"Leave him alone!" Lord Leile commanded. "We can summon him when the duke returns. We know where to find him."

Lord Neave set off to find his horse, almost overwhelmed with distress. Somehow he found his way to his mount and climbed into the saddle. Then he galloped away, heading for home.

THE DEPARTURE of Lord Neave did not end the turmoil in the council meeting.

"All of us like Lord Neave," said Lord Dunnridge reasonably. "But how can we do nothing, given what has happened?"

"No one has found Lord Neave guilty," Lord Storr insisted.

"No," Dunnridge replied. "Nevertheless, he stands accused by two witnesses. If we fail to take any action at all, we could reasonably stand accused ourselves—of countenancing treason."

"What are you proposing?" Lord Leile demanded.

"I acknowledge that it's reasonable to allow Lord Neave to return home to set his affairs in order. But he shouldn't be left there indefinitely. We should bring him into custody until the matter is resolved," Dunnridge replied.

Lord Leile scowled. "And who do you think is going to bring him in?"

"It should be done in a respectful and orderly manner. You yourself should name a leader, Lord Leile. Someone you trust. I have soldiers who are reliable. I would be happy to place some of them under the authority of whichever man you choose."

The morning dragged on as the issue continued to be hotly debated. Very few of the lords believed that Lord Neave was guilty, and many of them questioned the motivation behind the accusations of Lords Asturle and Dunnridge. But all acknowledged that the social order needed to be upheld and the rule of law maintained. And the processes associated with those imperatives must be respected.

Noon came and went, and Dunnridge's reasoning finally prevailed. A small majority of the lords agreed to bring Lord Neave into protective custody. The handling of it required considerable delicacy, and they reluctantly agreed to follow the approach proposed by Dunnridge.

The meeting then broke up in chaos. Most of the lords left with heavy hearts.

As promised, Lord Dunnridge wasted no time in assigning a squad of soldiers to assist in the task of bringing in Lord Neave. Lord Leile had appointed his own nephew, Dominic, to lead the squad. Dominic was widely known as a mature and reliable leader with a reputation for discretion. He was held in high esteem by all of the lords. The soldiers under his command would depart at noon on the following day.

Soon after dawn the next morning, Dunnridge sought out the squad of soldiers he had contributed to the expedition. They had their own leader—a man called Fowkes—one of Dunnridge's longest standing retainers and one of the few men Dunnridge trusted implicitly. Fowkes was also a ruthless killer.

The squad assigned to Fowkes was reliable, just as Dunnridge had promised. Their reliability, however, lay solely in their willingness to do whatever their leader deemed necessary to further the interests of Dunnridge.

"The situation has not developed quite as I expected," Dunnridge told Fowkes after briefing him. "And yet we now find ourselves with an extraordinary opportunity.

"Lord Neave must not be allowed to survive this exercise. I am relying on you to ensure that he is killed, supposedly while actively resisting the attempt to bring him in. His infant son must also die—

both outcomes are equally crucial. Do not fail me in this! While you're at it, take the opportunity to get rid of his woman, too. Her brazen independence is an affront to every noblewoman in the land —the very sight of her makes me want to vomit.

"I expect most of your squad to be killed in the process. It's a necessary sacrifice—I will not hold you responsible."

The squad leader grunted his understanding.

"Leile's nephew is an obstacle—we cannot afford to let him get in the way. As soon as you reach Neave's lands, dispose of him. We'll blame his death on Neave."

"Understood. It will happen exactly as you've said," Fowkes assured him.

"I'm also arranging for Asturle to be removed," Dunnridge told him. "He will be dealt with separately. That will also be blamed on Neave. The story will be that Neave decided to avenge himself on his accusers."

With his instructions in place, the squad leader bowed and departed. Dunnridge had no doubt that he would follow through on his orders meticulously.

Dunnridge left satisfied. Everything was progressing very well indeed—even better than he could have imagined.

THE SUN WAS NEARING the horizon when some sixth sense sent Lady Neave outside the house. As a result she was on hand to greet her husband when he reached home. Both he and his horse were clearly spent, and she was shocked by his ashen appearance.

"What's happened? Why are you home so soon?"

"I have been accused of treason! By Asturle and Dunnridge."

"What?! That makes no sense!"

"They're claiming I've been secretly plotting to discredit the duke."

She shook her head in complete bewilderment.

"The council allowed me to leave. But they'll almost certainly come for me. They can't afford to have someone at large with such serious charges hanging over them."

"But no one will believe it, surely!"

"It doesn't matter whether they believe it or not. There are processes that need to be followed. Dunnridge understands that perfectly. It's now clear why he wanted Asturle under his thumb."

She shook her head again. It was hard to credit that such a thing could be happening. Dunnridge was ambitious, and he was an opportunist. But why had he turned on her husband?

Perhaps Billson had some answers.

"Billson has returned," she said. "He's asked to see you as soon as you're available."

"I will meet with him as a matter of urgency. I need to find out whatever he's discovered. I must write to the duke while I still can, to make my case. Billson's information could be crucial."

"I will send for him."

"I am going to find Father Bryan. I will be back within the hour."

Her husband's words brought to mind the old cleric's warning. *Do not put your hope in princes, My Lady.* Had Father Bryan received some kind of premonition?

LADY NEAVE LOCATED BILLSON, and the two of them were waiting for Lord Neave when he returned.

Her husband's demeanor showed a greater measure of calm than when he had first arrived. Outwardly she, too, was calm, although she felt as if her insides had turned to ice.

Lord Neave wasted no time in addressing Billson. "Did you uncover anything?"

"Yes, My Lord! One of Lord Asturle's men apparently doesn't know how to keep his mouth shut when he gets a few drinks into him. If hearsay is to be believed, he boasted that he'd helped Lord Asturle poison his father."

The astonishment on the face of her husband mirrored her own reaction. "Do you think these reports are true?" she asked.

"I believe so, My Lady. I spoke to more than one witness who heard him say it. The accomplice himself has disappeared. He was seen in the company of some of Lord Dunnridge's men. It seems that Lord Dunnridge had need of his services."

Lord Neave nodded. "Thank you, Billson—you have done well. A number of things have become very clear."

He dismissed Billson and waited until he had gone.

"Now I know why Asturle was so terrified," he told her. "And to think I offered to help him! The young fool deserves to be hung!"

He paced back and forth, speechless with anger. With great difficulty she masked her own feelings, determined for his sake to stay strong.

He finally found his voice again. "Dunnridge clearly found out what he'd done—he's a manipulative schemer, and he loves nothing better than to dig up skeletons. He obviously threatened Asturle with exposure if he didn't agree to support his lies."

"What are you going to do?"

"Tomorrow I will write to the duke. Right now I'm going to sleep, if that's at all possible. I'm exhausted, and I'll need a clear head in the morning."

She drew him into her arms and held him tightly, desperate to find a way to melt the icicles that had encased her heart. Then she released him, and watched helplessly as he trudged away to his bed.

———

THE TROOP finally arrived at the boundary of Lord Neave's lands late on the day after Lord Neave's return. They had wasted no time.

Dunnridge's squad leader, Fowkes, was finding his mission much more difficult than he had expected. To begin with, Dominic, the nephew of Lord Leile and the person assigned to lead the expedition, had not come alone. He had brought six of his own soldiers, not many fewer than Fowkes's dozen. To make matters worse, Dominic clearly did not trust either Fowkes or his men. Thus far he had made sure that he was surrounded at all times by his own squad. And to cap it off, Dominic's men had the look of fighters. They would not easily be disposed of.

Fowkes had no solution in mind for these difficulties yet, but he was not alarmed. Experience had taught him that opportunities always appeared sooner or later. He simply needed to be ready to grasp them.

When the right moment arrived he would not hesitate. He was prepared to be utterly ruthless.

Lord Neave had spent the morning wrestling with his letter to the duke. When his wife arrived with refreshments, she found him destroying the document.

"What are you doing?" she asked with surprise.

He clenched his teeth in frustration. "For some strange reason I believed this was going to be a simple task. It's been much harder than I expected, and it's taken far too long. I finally got something written down, but then I stopped and read it through. I need it to be clear and convincing, but it just sounded petulant. The only thing I can do is start over."

"You can't expect to be your usual calm and persuasive self," she told him soothingly. "Not under these circumstances. Take your time and try again. You can't rush it."

She left him in peace and headed outside.

Lady Neave had herself been busy. She had risen before dawn to begin preparations of her own. As the sun rose she had sent for Hydin and Yosef.

When they arrived she took them aside. "Lord Neave has been falsely accused of serious misdeeds by the Lords Dunnridge and Asturle," she told them. "I don't know what they might be planning, but it wouldn't surprise me if one of them tries to take advantage of the situation. We need to be ready in case that happens."

Yosef had said nothing. He seemed no more surprised than if she'd told him the cows were being milked.

Hydin had simply nodded. "How can we help, My Lady?"

"I want thirty men on hand in case there is trouble. Hydin, I'm placing you in charge. Yosef, I'm relying on you to help Hydin. Do whatever he needs you to do. Work together to find the right men. I don't want any hotheads among them. They need to be confident with a sword, and at least some of them need to be good with a bow.

"Once you choose them, make sure they're properly armed and have plenty of food and water on hand. They might be in for a long wait.

"Then get them out of sight. I need them ready at a moment's notice, but I don't want them anywhere obvious or visible. We'll avoid fighting unless there's no other alternative. Make sure there are horses available, too, in case we need to move men quickly."

"When will Lord Neave review the men?" asked Hydin.

"He won't be reviewing them. He's busy, but he's also the person who's been accused. He can't be seen ordering men to fight, no matter what happens."

"Who will give the orders then, My Lady?" asked Yosef.

"I will."

If either of them were surprised, they didn't show it.

"We will not let you down, My Lady," Hydin told her.

He was as good as his word. By mid afternoon all of the men were in position.

3

"Agroup of riders is approaching, My Lady."

"How many?"

"About twenty."

"Notify Hydin. Then call for Lord Neave."

It had come so soon. She had been expecting it and done everything she could to prepare for it, but the news nevertheless felt like a physical blow to her gut.

Lord Neave joined her and together they walked outside to meet the riders.

"Did you finish the letter?" she asked him.

"Yes. I've entrusted it to Billson. He will leave in the morning to deliver it."

The sun was sinking low in the horizon, but they could clearly see the men as they approached.

"They've sent Dominic," she said.

Lord Neave nodded. "He's a good man."

A few of the new arrivals stayed close to Dominic. They threw frequent glances back at the rest, who rode a few horse lengths behind. As Dominic approached the manor house, Lady Neave noticed a couple of men peel off from the rear group and head in the direction of the barns.

Dominic rode up and dismounted. "Lord Neave," he said, dipping his head respectfully. "I have been asked to bring you to Maranelle."

Lord Neave nodded. "I have been expecting this. Can I offer you my sword?"

Dominic appraised him silently for a moment. "I appreciate the gesture, My Lord, but it will not be necessary. Not for the moment."

Lord Neave bowed in acknowledgment of Dominic's courtesy. "It is late. Will you accept our hospitality for the night? We can set off in the morning."

Dominic glanced briefly back at the larger group of men, who continued to hang back.

"I believe you plan to come willingly, Lord Neave," he observed.

"Yes. I understand the need for the process of law."

"Then I think it might be wiser if we leave immediately. And I would be grateful if some of your armed men could accompany us. A substantial group if possible."

Lord Neave looked at him questioningly.

"Unfortunately I was not offered the opportunity to select all of the men in our party," Dominic explained. "Some of those riding with us were provided by Lord Dunnridge. They are nominally under my command, but in practice they answer only to one of their own— a man known as Fowkes. I cannot speak for them."

At that moment a member of the other group dismounted and approached them. He came to a halt beside Dominic and bowed briefly. "My name is Fowkes," he said.

To Lady Neave the newcomer appeared calm and respectful. But a sudden sneer crossed his lips, changing his demeanor entirely. With a single fluid motion he leaned swiftly toward Dominic and sank a knife into his side, twisting it viciously on the way out.

She stood gaping in shock, her mouth open wide.

Fowkes stepped back from Dominic as his victim crumpled to the ground.

Dominic's men shouted in alarm, drawing their weapons hastily as they prepared to defend themselves.

Chaos erupted. The men from Fowkes's group leaped from their horses and attacked Dominic's men. Confusion reigned as knots of men struggled back and forth. Cries of fear and anger mingled with the clash of weapons and the anguished groans of the wounded.

Lady Neave watched on in horror as her peaceful garden was transformed into a killing ground. Lord Neave pushed her back toward the house. As she went, she shouted at the top of her voice, calling to her servants. "Summon Hydin!"

The chaos spread further afield as faint cries arose from the direction of the barns. She watched with narrowed eyes as tongues of flame rose, first from one barn, then from another. The pair who had detached themselves from Fowkes's group had been busy.

Hydin entered the fray at last. Horsemen galloped toward the barns to deal with the intruders, and Hydin himself rode up, surrounded by a large contingent of men.

Stranger battled stranger before the house. It was impossible for Lady Neave to distinguish between friend and foe. She realized at once that Hydin would have no more idea than she did. "Protect Lord Neave," she called.

Hydin and his men responded immediately, forming a defensive circle around their lord and his lady.

As they did so, the fighting came to an abrupt end. Lady Neave was not sure which side had won.

It quickly became obvious.

Fowkes shouted, "Lord Neave has murdered Dominic and his men! Avenge them!" Fowkes immediately led a savage attack on Lord Neave and his protectors. In the confusion Lady Neave was separated from her husband.

The intruders were outnumbered, but Hydin's men were unprepared for the reckless ferocity of Fowkes's attack. Two of the defenders were quickly slain, and Lady Neave watched with horror as Fowkes drove through her husband's guard and cut him down.

At once Fowkes called to his men—now reduced to four in

number—and they retreated hastily. As they mounted and rode off, Hydin's archers sent arrows streaking after them. Two riders tumbled from their saddles. Fowkes galloped away with his two remaining companions.

Hydin's men began to mill about aimlessly, wide-eyed and breathing heavily.

The fugitives were disappearing into the distance, and before long darkness would conspire to cover their escape.

"After them!" Hydin shouted in exasperation. Several of his men hurriedly found mounts and set off in pursuit.

Lady Neave cared nothing for any of it. She knelt beside the body of her husband, overcome with grief.

Then one of her maids approached, her face covered with tears. "My Lady!" she cried. "Your son!"

Lady Neave looked up, uncomprehending. Then with her heart pounding in her chest, she flew inside, crying out for her child. "Donnie! Donnie!"

She ran to his room and burst through the door. What awaited her was beyond nightmare. She stumbled to her knees, retching violently.

The lifeless body of her son lay sprawled on the floor. His nurse lay beside him. His carer, stouthearted to the last, had clearly given her life in a futile attempt to protect the child.

Lady Neave collapsed, no longer able to will her muscles to function.

THE NIGHT DRAGGED by in an agonizing daze for Lady Neave. She had known sorrow and loss, but for the most part her life had been a happy one. She had loved and respected her husband and adored their child. The Neave holdings were prosperous and their retainers content. She had embraced her role as lady of the estate enthusiastically, and her personal life had been enriched by the simple joys associated with caring for her little family.

That world had just ended abruptly. Should death have visited her in the night she would have embraced it gladly.

Eventually the hours of darkness passed. Inexplicably, the sun rose, and the birds sang as they always had.

She knew there were things she ought to attend to—her responsibilities as noblewoman had not ended. But she could muster neither the energy nor the motivation to leave her room. Food was brought to her, but she ignored it. She could not imagine eating when her insides were knotted so tightly.

Late in the morning Father Bryan appeared in her room. "You are needed, My Lady," he said. Without asking for permission, he firmly but gently took her by the arm and guided her outside, into the blinding light of day. She followed him resignedly, accepting reluctantly that she had shut out the world for long enough.

The sight of a row of freshly dug graves brought an end to her self absorption. The pressing priority was to bury the dead, and men had been hard at work for several hours in preparation. She quickly saw that Father Bryan had overseen the work.

He pointed to the graves. "Out of respect for Dominic we have prepared a separate grave for him. We plan to bury the other intruders in a common grave, friend and foe together. We have no way of being certain which of the men came with Dominic anyway," he explained.

She nodded dully.

"Separate plots have been dug for each of our own men who were killed." He pointed to four freshly dug graves.

"Lord Neave and your son will be laid to rest in the family crypt nearby," he concluded.

"Thank you, Father," she said, forcing her words past the tightness in her jaw.

"It was the least I could do, My Lady." He bowed, his wrinkled face softened by concern.

A small crowd slowly gathered, and they fell silent as Father Bryan pronounced the burial rites. He reminded them of the sacrificial death of their savior, and the defeat of death through his resurrection. He spoke of the promise of eternal life and the certainty of a final reckoning.

Then he stood before the graves of the intruders. "We do not stand in judgment of these men—only God can judge them. And he will. He does not ignore evil—each of us will be held accountable for the way we have lived our lives."

Father Bryan moved to the graves of the locals. "These men were our friends," he said. "We knew them, and we knew their character. As we grieve for them, let us not forget the joyful times we shared together. The memory of them will live on in every person touched by their lives."

Finally, he stood before the graves of Lord Neave and his son. "Our time on earth is but a moment in the span of eternity. Our beloved Lord Neave's time on earth is over, but his life has not ended. He is with his Lord." He paused, closing his eyes momentarily.

Then he continued slowly, with sorrow evident on his face. "I do not pretend to understand why a much loved two-year old was taken from us. Some mysteries will one day be explained, but only by the Almighty."

He directed his gaze to those around him before bringing it to rest on Lady Neave. "The most difficult path is walked by those who remain. There is release, though, in our tears. There is no shame in grief. We heal as we express our grief."

Father Bryan's words reached her ears, but they did not penetrate her heart. She did not want to heal. How could she ever become comfortable with the deaths of her beloved husband and her precious son? Surely doing so could only diminish their memory.

If grieving led to healing, she would not grieve. If tears led to release, she would never weep. Her commitment to the memory of those she had loved would be to refuse to ever let them go.

At that moment something hardened inside her. From the instant she'd caught sight of her son's body, she had been swept along in the tide of her emotions. No longer. She would rule her feelings ruthlessly; she would not be subject to them. Whenever her emotions attempted to surface, she would force them back down.

Rather than untangling the tight knot within her spirit, she decided to make a truce with it. She would not attempt to rid herself of her pain. Why should she go free when those she loved had drunk the bitter cup to the dregs?

Perhaps from that moment she would lead a diminished life, but she had at least discovered a way to face the world again.

BEFORE THE SUN WENT DOWN, Lady Neave had begun to take charge of the affairs of the estate. Her people deferred to her, partly out of sympathy and partly because of her rank. Beyond all of that, they recognized in her a capable and trustworthy leader.

As soon as she once again directed her attention beyond her own four walls, she realized that her troubles were far from over. Without a way of refuting the charges against her husband, it was likely that his lands would be declared forfeit. Had his heir survived, the estate might have been held over in trust until the boy came of age. With both of them gone, though, Dunnridge would undoubtedly focus his energies on finding a way to force her out.

Her husband's letter was the key to clearing his name, and she searched everywhere for it. He had told her that he'd entrusted it to Billson, the same person who gathered evidence about Lord Asturle's murder of his father. But in a perverse twist of fate, Billson had become one of the few casualties among the Neave retainers in the fighting. She searched his dwelling and among his few possessions, but there was no sign of the letter. She searched her husband's study, too, but he did not appear to have made a copy.

She finally gave up and went to her bed. The missing letter nagged incessantly at her, but she had no idea what to do about it. The parchment had simply vanished.

IN THE CAPITAL OF MARANELLE, Lord Dunnridge listened to Fowkes's detailed report with considerable satisfaction.

"You have entirely repaid my confidence in you, Fowkes. You will be richly rewarded!"

His underling bowed. "There is one other minor matter, My Lord," he said. He handed the nobleman a folded parchment. "This was found by Solly."

Dunnridge took it and examined it briefly. It clearly bore the seal of Lord Neave. "Where did it come from?" he asked, frowning.

"When we escaped from Neave's holdings we took the first horses we could find. It was in the saddlebag of the horse Solly was riding."

The seal had not been broken. Nevertheless Dunnridge asked him suspiciously, "Do you know what it says?"

Fowkes shrugged. "I can't read, My Lord. Nor can Solly."

Dunnridge nodded, satisfied. He broke open the seal and unfolded the parchment. Then he read it rapidly, a frown of concentration on his brow.

When he finished he folded the document and secured it safely within his gown. "Gather fifty men and return to Neave's holdings. Don't delay! Burn it all to the ground—the house, the barns, everything. Bring back the spoils. Eliminate Neave's retainers, especially any who are armed. And don't return this time until the woman is dead!"

Fowkes bowed and departed.

As soon as he once again found himself alone, Dunnridge began pacing around the room, awash with nervous energy. Finally he stopped and let out an exultant whoop of pure glee. Intercepting the parchment was an incredible stroke of luck. Neave's letter—had it ever been delivered to the duke—could have caused serious problems for Dunnridge. The writing was factual, believable, and carefully reasoned. And it contained information with the potential to incriminate Asturle and completely undermine all of Dunnridge's scheming.

The fact that the letter existed at all sobered the nobleman considerably. He realized he had seriously underestimated his victim. Neave had done some careful digging of his own, and drawn some very shrewd conclusions.

Asturle's accomplice had also created more complications than Dunnridge expected. The fool had outlived his usefulness—he would not see another dawn.

There were lessons to be learned from this experience, and Dunnridge vowed to himself to never again leave so much to chance.

He found a candle and lit it. Then he retrieved the parchment from his cloak and carefully held it to the flame, not resting until nothing remained except ash.

It seemed unlikely that Neave had made a copy. But if he had, burning down his house and killing his woman should deal once and for all with any possibility of it surfacing.

***

Lady Neave rose with the dawn after tossing and turning restlessly throughout the night.

As the day wore away she made several fruitless attempts to find her husband's letter. It was nowhere to be found. She quickly recognized, though, that the document would no longer be sufficient, even if it did reappear. The council needed to be made aware of the actions of Dunnridge's men.

She knew roughly what her husband had intended to communicate. And she had witnessed first hand the murders of Dominic and his men and her husband. The following morning she would write a letter of her own and send it to the duke.

The afternoon was drawing to a close when one of her servants appeared at the door. "Hydin is requesting to see you, My Lady."

"Send him in."

Hydin entered the room and bowed. His face was grim. "We have a problem, My Lady."

She peered at him curiously. The magnitude of their problems was so self-evident that at first she didn't take him seriously. His demeanor soon caught her full attention.

"I took the liberty of posting scouts along the road to Maranelle. I hope I have not acted improperly." He looked anxious.

"Of course not! I should have thought of it myself. What's the problem?"

"A large body of armed men is heading in this direction. At least fifty of them. They wear the standard of Lord Dunnridge."

Her heart skipped a beat. "When will they reach us?"

"Given the late hour, they seem to have decided to set up camp. If they break camp at dawn, they will probably arrive by noon."

Her mind began to spin. They had so little time. Her emotions welled up, threatening to unhinge her completely. She gritted her teeth and thrust her feelings away determinedly.

This outcome was not entirely unexpected. It had occurred to her that Dunnridge might take matters into his own hands. She had not anticipated it so soon, though.

She considered the possibilities. Dunnridge's men were not coming to engage in dialogue, and the nobleman had sent a large enough force that she could not be confident of defeating them if it came to a fight. And even if they fought and her men emerged victorious, at what cost? Dunnridge might be willing to sacrifice his people, but she was not. More than enough bodies had been carried from her doorstep already.

The idea of writing a letter—so appealing such a short time ago —now seemed pointless. This new development showed it to be a waste of time.

The council clearly had no answer to the lies and maneuvering of Dunnridge. The nobles had sent an armed party to arrest her husband, even though he had done nothing wrong. Then Dunnridge had ordered the murder of Lord Neave on his own estate. The murder had been carried out openly, in broad daylight. The brazenness of it was breathtaking.

The nobles had proven themselves inept and powerless. If she sent one of her men to them with a letter, she would almost certainly be sending him to his death. If she appeared before the council herself, there was no telling what Dunnridge might do. Placing any hope in the council would be dangerous folly.

Now Dunnridge had sent more men. It could only be for one

reason—to eliminate every possible witness to his earlier treachery. She had nowhere to turn. She needed to act decisively, and she needed to do it now.

"Call together the people. All of them. I will address them within the hour."

Hydin left to carry out her instructions. She watched him go with somber musings.

Unprecedented situations called for unprecedented actions. She would allow her people to choose their own course.

She didn't imagine for a minute that offering them a choice was doing them a favor. All of them would struggle to accept such a freedom. The nobility decided for them. It had always been that way. But she intended to propose an unimaginable course of action. She could not in all good conscience force her people to accept it.

Her proposal would be difficult to stomach. Her people would soon discover, though, that there were no palatable options on the table.

LADY NEAVE STOOD before the gathered throng. Almost two hundred of them had crowded together to hear what she had to say. All of them were restless, and fear was evident on many faces. They had seen their peaceful existence shattered, and they were about to discover there was little likelihood of getting it back.

"I have not come to you with good news," she called out. "Evil men have first accused then murdered your lord, and their scheming is far from over. I believe they will not rest until everything we see around us lies in ruins. The death and destruction we have witnessed is not yet at an end. This is only the beginning.

"These men will punish you for defending your lord, even though you did no more than your duty. Even now a large body of armed men is coming here to finish what they started."

Loud murmuring broke out at her words.

"They will arrive before noon tomorrow," she continued.

"I will not ask you to fight them. I have no wish to see any more of you die. But I cannot allow you to stay and meet your fate, either. So I offer you two possible futures. Each family must decide for itself."

She paused to assess their reaction. The faces might be grim, but she knew they were made of stern stuff.

"I have decided to leave my comfortable home, and to bid farewell forever to the final resting place of those I loved." She took a deep breath and steadied herself, determined not to allow her bitterness to interfere with what she needed to say. "I will make my home in the wilderness, far from anyone who might seek advantage at our expense," she continued woodenly.

She paused again, only with effort succeeding in calming herself. "I have not decided this simply for my own sake. I have access to money and resources, and I have the means to slip away quietly to a distant country to preserve my own life. I am also doing it for the sake of all those who have faithfully served the Neave family for many generations. Anyone who wishes to can join me. You will be taking your chances in the wilderness, carving out a new home by the sweat of your brow. I will not pretend to you that it will be an easy task. But it will offer you an opportunity to remove yourselves far from strife.

"Anyone who wishes to stay here may do so. I have spoken to Father Bryan. He intends to continue to make his home here, and he is willing to offer his guidance to any who make the same decision. For any who decide against leaving, may your new masters prove themselves worthy of your service!

"It will not be safe for anyone to stay here tomorrow, though. You must leave temporarily, to preserve your lives.

"All of us will withdraw to a safe distance. We will watch and wait, and we will see what these men do. If they are marauders bent only on death and destruction, then those who wish to remain here must stay well clear of them until they are long gone. If, in spite of my expectations, their intention proves to be honorable, you may return to your homes immediately. And any who have previously decided to flee with me can choose to change their minds and stay instead."

She paused again, but only for a moment.

"Go now, all of you, and make your plans. Whether you decide to stay or to leave, gather sufficient provisions to last you many days. Wagons will be made available to transport your possessions and little ones. But you must plan to travel light.

"Choose carefully what to take with you. And be aware that anything you leave behind may soon be destroyed.

"We will meet again at dawn."

With that she dismissed them.

4

Lord Dunnridge stood solemnly before a hastily convened meeting of Erestor's Council of Lords. He calmly scanned the faces around him, a sober expression on his face. He nodded to Lord Leile. "Thank you for arranging this meeting, My Lord. I have grave news to report." He paused for effect.

Lord Leile was not in a patient mood. "Get on with it!" he said testily.

Lord Dunnridge bowed. "As you know, this council sent a squad to bring Lord Neave back to Maranelle. They were capably led by a respected commander, and they proceeded with restraint and moderation as instructed. I am sorry to say that Lord Neave aggressively resisted their efforts. His intransigence led to a battle, and the result has been a significant loss of life." He turned to face Lord Leile. "I regret to inform you that your nephew has been killed, My Lord, along with all of the men who traveled with him. A number of my own retainers also accompanied your nephew—over a dozen of them. Only three have returned."

His words were greeted with uproar, and it was some minutes before Lord Leile was able to restore order.

"What of Lord Neave?"

"It need hardly be said that Lord Neave bears a heavy burden of responsibility for what happened. It nevertheless pains me to inform you that he was killed in the fighting."

Many of the lords were instantly on their feet, all shouting at once. This time it took longer for the pandemonium to settle. In the end Lord Leile shouted them down. "My Lords, I will end this meeting now if this chaos continues!"

The lords gradually resumed their seats, although loud muttering continued unabated.

Lord Dunnridge continued. "I regret to report that Lord Neave's young son was also killed in the confusion."

This latest news was greeted with stunned silence.

"This particular outcome is especially grievous," the nobleman continued. "The boy was in no way responsible for his father's actions, and I have no doubt that with wise guidance he could eventually have taken his father's place on this council."

"But why would Neave behave in this way?" asked Lord Storr. "It makes no sense!"

"Perhaps you are forgetting his treason," Lord Dunnridge replied. "When cornered, guilty men can prove themselves capable of surprising behavior."

"What of Lady Neave?" asked Lord Leile.

"A new report has only just reached me, and it contained possibly the most surprising and disappointing news of all. In a shameless effort to shield those who murdered our men, Lady Neave has destroyed her own home and fled with the killers. She has, in effect, declared herself outlaw."

As the lords began to erupt once again, Lord Leile rose to his feet and thumped the table repeatedly. The men subsided, although many of them were unable to suppress their agitation.

"Where has she gone?" Lord Leile asked.

"I do not yet know," Lord Dunnridge replied, "although I have sent men with orders to bring her in. Alive, of course, since she must answer for her actions."

"By what authority have you ordered such a measure?" Lord Leile demanded, his face red with anger.

"I will recall my men instantly since Your Lordship disapproves," Dunnridge replied placatingly. "Perhaps I was overly hasty, given my own very personal stake in this matter—ten of my men were killed by Lord Neave's butchers."

"Recall your men," Lord Leile demanded, "and do it now! No further action of any kind will be taken without the full agreement of this council! We already have enough of a catastrophe to deal with."

Lord Dunnridge bowed low to signal his acquiescence.

"Where is Lord Asturle?" asked Lord Storr, looking around him. "Why isn't he here?"

"There is to be no end of bad news, it seems," Lord Leile responded grimly. "His body was found this morning beside the main road to Maranelle. It appears that he was murdered."

This report was greeted with further cries of dismay.

Lord Dunnridge sighed deeply. "That is heavy news indeed. It is rumored that Lord Neave ordered his assassination, presumably in revenge for Lord Asturle's testimony against him. It seems that those reports were more than just rumors."

"This is not the time for speculation," Lord Leile declared irritably. "This meeting is at an end. When he returns, the duke will decide where to go from here."

Most of the lords left the council meeting with grim faces and downcast eyes.

Only Lord Dunnridge emerged satisfied. He departed very satisfied indeed.

"Our scouts have returned, My Lady."

Lady Neave nodded, joining Hydin as he led her toward the two men who had just dismounted. She glanced up at the sky as they walked—the thick pall of smoke that had appeared to the northwest removed any element of mystery from their report.

The scouts bowed as she approached. They were clearly distressed. "They've torched the buildings, My Lady," one of them told her. "Our homes, the manor house, the outbuildings, the remaining barns—everything. By tomorrow morning there'll be no sign that anyone lived there."

"And they're slaughtering anything that moves!" the other scout added. "Cattle, sheep, pigs, goats, chickens." He shook his head in bafflement.

"Thank you for your report," she replied. "Their intentions are now perfectly clear. Please spread the news. The people need to be told."

She turned to Hydin. "We cannot afford to stay here. We need to get further away—much further away—and we need to move quickly."

***

Lady Neave and her people were in deep trouble. After days of headlong flight they had somehow managed to stay ahead of their pursuers. Barely. They had traveled by night as well as by day. They had also won a little time thanks to carefully selected ambush locations that allowed their best archers to pick off Dunnridge's scouts before fleeing quickly away.

Now their enemies had almost run them to ground. Only a mountain pass lay between them. It was sufficiently narrow in places that the exhausted fugitives had barely succeeded in bringing their wagons through.

Flight was no longer an option—they had to stand and fight.

Perhaps it would all end right there. They had no intention of making it easy, though. A last-ditch plan had hastily been implemented.

"They're coming through!" hissed Yosef.

Lady Neave nodded sharply to Hydin. As their pursuers spurred their horses forward into the pass, he raised his hand, signaling the men to move into position.

The riders were gradually forced into single file as the pass narrowed. The lead riders had barely emerged from the other end when a loud rumbling sound began. Every one of the riders looked up. The sound grew in volume as a large rock came crashing down from the top of the pass, dislodging other rocks as it fell. More rocks soon followed, triggering an avalanche. Several of the horsemen disappeared from sight, buried beneath a pile of rocks. The pass was sealed not far from its entrance.

Ten riders were now trapped, separated from their companions. Before they could recover from their surprise a rain of arrows began to descend on them. Some shafts missed the riders completely, but others picked out their targets with deadly accuracy.

Desperate to escape the lethal rain, the surviving riders urged their horses forward out of the pass. Three more fell to a final flurry of arrows as they broke free, then the riders were set upon from all sides. A fierce hand-to-hand battle ensued.

Not for the first time, Lady Neave wished she could join them in the battle. Nevertheless, she watched with growing satisfaction as, outnumbered and cut off, the invaders fell one by one. The last of them was a big brute of a man. Hydin spurred his horse toward him resolutely. Both of them were mounted, and the horses twisted and turned as their riders traded blows. In the confusion a deflected stroke took Hydin across the face, and blood flowed freely from a wound over his eye.

Hydin did not lose his nerve. He could not match the strength of the bigger man, but he possessed the greater skill. Patiently he waited for his opportunity. When his opponent took a mighty swing and overreached, Hydin leaned forward with a precise thrust, penetrating the big man's guard. He didn't try to hide his relief as his enemy slipped from the saddle.

Hydin sat impassively while his face was being stitched, assessing the outcome with Lady Neave. "Did we lose anyone, My Lady?" he asked.

"We lost two," she replied, hardening herself in an effort to keep her distress from showing. "Several others are wounded, but fortunately their injuries are mostly minor."

Hydin winced, and not from his wound. "We can't afford to lose more people!" he groaned.

"But we did account for thirteen or fourteen of them," Yosef told him.

"You can add three more to that tally." The quietly spoken words came from Hender, a young man who had quickly emerged as the best of the archers. "I climbed to the top of the pass and picked off some of their men on the other side. They scrambled out of range before I could take their leader."

"If you were able to climb the pass, then they can do it too," Hydin said grimly.

"Not with their horses," Hender replied with a tight smile.

"No, they won't find it easy," agreed Lady Neave.

"We can afford to rest for a moment," she said. "We've lost friends today. That's painful. The harsh reality is that we will almost certainly sustain further losses in the future. Nevertheless, you've all done extraordinarily well!

"To begin with, we managed to induce them to follow us. That means that the friends and family who decided not to join us are now far behind, and quite safe. That's an important achievement, especially since almost all of the fighting men came with us, leaving them largely unprotected.

"Your efforts here at the pass have also reduced their numbers significantly. And you've taught them not to underestimate us."

"The plan was yours, My Lady!" said Hydin.

"You made it work," she countered.

She glanced up at the sky. "It's getting late. We need to move again soon. They'll eventually find a way through, and we need to be long gone when that happens."

"Maybe they'll give up after what just happened," Yosef said hopefully.

Lady Neave shook her head. She didn't need a magical talisman to know what these men were intending. "I don't understand the reason behind it, but it's becoming clear to me that these men are not going to quit. They'll follow us to the bitter end, whether it's our end or their own."

THE ONLY REALITY the fugitives now recognized was the struggle of their unending flight. The constant strain had brought them almost to breaking point. Lady Neave knew they couldn't continue for much longer.

They had traveled southeast for days, going to extreme lengths to avoid being seen. Fortunately, inhabited areas were few and far between in this part of the country. They had given each of them a wide berth.

Only once had they encountered a major road—the road that led from Maranelle to Steffan's Citadel. Weary of forever hiding, Lady Neave had decided to take a risk. She waited until midnight had passed, then she directed them onto the road. The moon was hidden entirely in clouds, and the wind howled unrelentingly. It was not a night for traveling. They had seen no one.

After hurrying east along the road for several hours, they headed south again into the mountains. They had made excellent time.

They must have picked the wrong place to leave the road, though. It now appeared that they were trapped.

"There's nowhere to go, My Lady. Ahead of us is a huge lake, with no obvious way past it. If we turn aside they'll catch us in the open."

"Why can't we get past the lake?"

"One side is completely inaccessible. The other side has a steep slope beside the lake that looks very unstable in places. There are rocks at the top of the slope, but we won't be able to climb across them. Even without the horses they're impassable."

"Has Hydin taken a look at it?"

"I'm not sure, My Lady. He isn't here right now."

At that very moment, someone called, "Scar's just ridden in."

There it was again. Hydin had a name, but suddenly everyone was calling him Scar.

She had found herself reacting to the nickname at first, but he seemed contented enough with the change. He wore his battle wound almost as a trophy, a symbol of defiance. Yes, that was it. The scar had become a symbol—a token of triumph over adversity. Her people needed symbols.

"Tell Scar I need to see him," she said.

A LINE of refugees stretched along the fringe of the lake. Lady Neave had decided to risk the slope. It was an easy decision in the end, because they had no real choice. They had been forced to abandon the wagons, and anything they couldn't carry had been left behind. The women and children went first, led by Yosef. With the slope too unstable for rapid movement, progress had been painfully slow.

"Scar and Hender, the rest of us are about to leave, but I need you to stay here. Get out of sight. Once they're all onto the slope, find a safe location where you can pick them off from behind. One way or another, this ends here, right now. Make good use of your bows. I don't expect you will need to use your swords.

"They outnumber us—they must still have thirty men at least. And they're men without conscience. It will be a brutal fight. We need to gain any advantage we can from the terrain, along with your harassment from the rear."

The two men nodded, and set off to find a suitable place to await the imminent arrival of their foes.

By the time the pursuers reached the lake, Lady Neave and her fighters were more than halfway across the slope that bordered the lake. It had been necessary for them to move with extreme caution. Many of them had slipped and slid, one or two of them almost to the surface of the lake.

One section of the slope was especially unstable. As soon as they were beyond it, they took up positions and waited. Lady Neave knew that her bowmen gave them an edge, but the fighting so far suggested that Dunnridge's men were better trained with the sword. If it came to hand-to-hand fighting...she couldn't bring herself to think about it.

She didn't have to wait long before their pursuers appeared. There was no forward rush this time. They paused and assessed the situation thoroughly before any of them set out across the slope. She recognized Fowkes among them, shouting orders from the rear. He had clearly learned caution in recent days. His wariness apparently didn't extend to the mounted men he was driving forward onto the slope ahead of him, though.

As soon as her enemies had entered the most unstable section, Lady Neave nodded to her archers, and they let loose a steady stream of arrows. Few of the bowmen beside her could match the skill of Hender or Scar or Yosef, but the arrows nevertheless began to take a toll.

"Get moving!" Fowkes bellowed.

His men surged forward obediently. The result was immediate disaster. Riders lost their seats as the ground gave way completely beneath their horses. Lady Neave watched wide-eyed as the confusion spread. Dismounted men in turn lost their footing, slipping and slithering down the slope, tormented by a persistent hail of arrows.

Most of the men soon found themselves in the water. She saw at once that few of them were able to swim. Some tried to cling to horses, only to be shaken loose in the thrashing turmoil. The futile struggle for survival below her was too terrible to watch, and she averted her gaze involuntarily.

The few who made it to the bank were picked off one at a time by the archers. After all her people had endured at the hands of their enemies, the merciless response of her bowmen did not shock her. She made no attempt to restrain them.

It was all over in a few frantic minutes. Six men remained on the slope, Fowkes among them. The survivors wasted no time retreating from the lake, chased off by loud taunts as well as a final flurry of arrows as they rode away.

At that moment Hender and Scar appeared in their path. As the riders spurred their horses toward them, the two archers calmly nocked and released arrow after arrow. Men and horses came crashing down, but the gap was narrowing rapidly. Lady Neave looked on with growing anxiety. Then the last of the riders were upon the bowmen.

Scar and Hender drew their swords as soon as their enemies drew too close for archery. Their efforts had not been in vain. Only two men remained, both having lost their mounts moments earlier. One was Fowkes. He was limping from an arrow that still protruded from his leg.

Fowkes's companion ran at Hender, and the two combatants were quickly lost to sight behind a rocky outcrop as they fought.

At the same moment Fowkes assaulted Scar. Lady Neave gasped in fear as her husband's killer surged to the attack, moving as though he wasn't injured.

A deadly dance ensued as Fowkes and Scar struggled back and forth. Fowkes lunged forward repeatedly, with Scar barely managing to stay out of his reach.

Scar did not entirely yield the initiative, though. Once, twice, three times his sword flicked out, cutting the big man but not disabling him. Fowkes's rage grew with his pain.

Greatly alarmed, Lady Neave gestured to her men to go to Scar's support. She moved forward with them.

She watched with increasing perplexity as the battle unfolded. Scar seemed to be making no attempt to finish off his enemy.

Then, in a moment of shock, she understood. He had no intention of ending it quickly. He was toying with Fowkes. He was playing an extremely dangerous game, but his face showed nothing but calm resolve.

Her men finally drew near as Fowkes suddenly tripped and fell. Scar raised a hand to forestall them. "He's mine!" he said coolly.

Scar allowed Fowkes to clamber to his feet, then he stretched forward and plunged his blade into the killer's side, beneath his leather jerkin. "That's for Dominic," he said.

Fowkes stumbled, but kept his feet. Scar's blade flicked forward again, taking Fowkes in the neck. "That's for Lord Neave," he said.

This time Fowkes crashed to the ground. He lay wide-eyed and unmoving on his back. Scar stood over him and raised his sword high. Then he slowly and deliberately ran him through. "And that's for every other person you've killed for no good reason," he said between clenched teeth.

Lady Neave stood stunned, unwilling to trust herself to speak. Her agitation had grown as she witnessed Scar's drawn out and remorseless execution of Fowkes. The killer had murdered Dominic and her husband before her very eyes, and ordered the deaths of her son and so many others. Now he had finally been repaid, in kind.

Her emotions almost burst free of their restraints. Exerting all her willpower she contained them, refusing even to acknowledge her own emotional response.

The sudden reappearance of Hender restored her equilibrium. He staggered in and came to a halt, breathing heavily. "I finished it," he said, answering the question in their eyes.

She stood frozen, struggling to believe that it was over.

It wasn't a dream, though. No one was pursuing them any more. No one even knew where they were.

It was truly over.

EPILOGUE

Lady Neave followed Scar through the trees. "We're almost there, My Lady," he said.

She stepped forward and gasped with surprise and wonder.

She found herself standing in the largest natural clearing she had ever seen. Hidden deep within the forest, it was surrounded by ancient trees of great girth, and bathed with the sunlight that flooded down through the opening to the sky above. The sense of calm and tranquility was almost palpable.

The bubbling of water sounded nearby. She walked across the clearing and stepped back among the trees. Almost immediately she came to a pleasant meadow beside a broad stream. Trout would almost certainly be lurking nearby.

She returned to the clearing and gazed slowly around it. They could build huts around its edges, and the open space was wide enough to easily allow for huge bonfires and community gatherings, even if their numbers increased significantly.

While she absorbed the atmosphere, the other refugees arrived, spilling into the open space. The awe on their faces told her all she needed to know.

"This is the place," she said, her voice hushed. She had lowered her voice almost instinctively—somehow it seemed fitting in the stillness among the majestic trees.

"How far are we from other settlements?" Scar asked the scouts.

"So far we've seen no sign of anyone within a couple of days ride," one of them replied.

"The hunting will be good," said Hender with a grin, sweeping his arm around the surrounding forest.

"Will the soil support farming?" someone asked.

"We will find out," Lady Neave replied. "If it doesn't, we will search out another place that's even further from human habitation. Somewhere with rich soil and good water.

"But for now, we will make our home here. We will build sturdy huts to see us through the winter, and we will hunt and fish, and seek out every available food source."

Her words were received enthusiastically. Animated conversations broke out everywhere around her. Relief was evident on all of their faces.

None of them could have anticipated the suffering and hardship they had been forced to endure. Along the way they had buried as many women and children as fighting men. The strain had been overwhelming.

But the journey was over at last.

She looked down at herself. Her once elegant garments were now tattered and stained. In so many ways she was no longer the person she used to be. The past had gone, and as far as she was concerned, it had gone forever. She had once walked as an equal among the aristocracy—the most celebrated men and women in the land. But her own had failed her. The nobility offered no justice to her husband, and no protection to her.

She thrust her resentment aside, determined not to be ruled by bitterness. She would leave the past behind her, whatever it took.

Hydin had adopted a new name. It was time she did the same.

"I have something to say to you all," she called loudly.

Conversation ceased abruptly, and all eyes turned in her direction.

"We have found the refuge we were seeking. It will be a place of safety, of new beginnings. We can rebuild our homes and our lives here.

"I will continue to lead you, for as long as you wish it. But I will no longer lead you as Lady Neave. I was given a name at my birth—Anneka —and from this moment I will answer to nothing else. There will be no more 'My Lady.' If you wish to show me respect, then call me by my name.

"That is all. I thank you."

She gazed for a moment across the sea of startled faces, then looked away. It would take them time to adjust, but they had already demonstrated remarkable flexibility.

They had arrived at last at a place where they could begin to put down deep roots. It was peaceful, it was beautiful, and in time it would become a thriving community.

It could never fill the aching void inside her, though. She could be their leader, she could be strong for them. But she could never regain here what she had lost. She had known joy, for a time. But it was beyond her reach now.

She looked around at their faces. She could sense that many of them were allowing themselves to hope again. A few even wore tentative smiles.

There was so much that needed to be done, but they would overcome the obstacles. She didn't doubt it. They would find a way, and they would do it together.

She knew that her people needed her, and she was willing to spend herself in serving them.

It was enough.

It would have to be enough.

The End

The story of Anneka and her community continues in
The Cost of Knowing,
Book Two of *The Stone Cycle*, by Allan N. Packer

Change brings new opportunity. Offered a chance to rediscover joy, Anneka
must choose whether or not to embrace it.

NOTE FROM THE AUTHOR

Thank you for reading *The Rending: A Prequel to The Cost of Knowing*—I hope you enjoyed it. Thank you, too, for joining my mailing list at *www.allanpacker.com*. If you have already read *The Cost of Knowing (The Stone Cycle Book 2)*, I trust that the novelette provided useful background to Anneka, her companions, and their refuge, along with a hint about the prehistory of the Stone of Knowing.

You can discover more about Anneka in *The Cost of Knowing* and subsequent books in *The Stone Cycle* series (the series comprises six full-length novels and a prequel novelette).

The Stone of Knowing and *The Cost of Knowing* are outlined below.

If you've finished *The Stone Cycle* series and you're ready for more, don't miss *The Hard Edge of Magic*, the opening novel in my new epic fantasy series, *The Ruptured Kingdom*! The novel is described below.

And, as a subscriber to my mailing list, you're very welcome to download a bonus copy of *The Renegade*, the novelette prequel to *The Hard Edge of Magic*. It is also described below. You should have received an email with a link to the novelette. Contact me if you can't find it.

Even a small stone creates big ripples

The untroubled world of young Thomas Stablehand is changed forever when he stumbles upon an unusual stone. With the thoughts and intents of others laid bare, he eagerly indulges his curiosity. But seeing into other minds isn't like Thomas expected. And troubles are only beginning.

When invaders attack the kingdom of Arvenon, Thomas has nowhere to turn except to his friend Will Prentis, a gifted and ambitious leader who has risen rapidly in the ranks of the king's army.

Will is fearless, and where he leads men follow. With the kingdom on the brink, Will leads a small band on a perilous quest to thwart the invaders. Fearing his secret will be exposed, and hoping to help prevent catastrophe, Thomas flees with them.

But dangerous enemies seek the stone for their own ends. As Will faces a relentless opponent whose true purpose remains hidden, Thomas must decide what price he's willing to pay to protect the stone and preserve the kingdom.

The ripples begin to make waves

Thomas Stablehand's life is not the only thing spinning out of control since he found the stone. Entire kingdoms are now in turmoil.

Will Prentis, newly appointed as army commander, must outmaneuver a growing array of enemies as he prepares for an unequal showdown with Arvenon's invaders. Thomas, hunted unceasingly, must sacrifice all to safeguard the stone.

The fate of kingdoms soon hinges on them as they confront a ruthless invader hiding a darker purpose.

The odds are hopeless. And for three kingdoms, the stakes are higher than anyone knows.

Hungry and desperate, Kylen knows what it's like to be an outcast. Plucked from the streets by a tight-lipped stranger, he begins to dream of a better life. But his rescuer turns out to be a renegade mage. In an instant Kylen finds himself transformed from a person of no account to a dangerous fugitive.

But much more than his life might be at stake. Dark forces are stirring, and an ancient evil is poised, ready to be unleashed on an unsuspecting kingdom. Comfortable and arrogant, the kingdom's mages are bent on destroying the one person capable of saving them.

On the run with his mentor, Kylen tries to ignore the voices whispering about his destiny. Of what use is a fabled destiny when you're struggling to survive?

Is anything worth being hunted and despised?

Dalthinir's life quickly unravels when he acts on suspicions about a fellow mage. After desperately using magic to escape an attempt on his life, he finds himself on trial for murder.

But more is at stake than his reputation. In their greed for power, reckless mages are willing to risk a release of magic so powerful it will destroy the kingdom. He alone recognizes the peril.

Prohibited from taking action, Dalthinir must decide what he is prepared to lose for the sake of the kingdom.

Can he sacrifice everything he cares about to become a scorned and hunted renegade?

Find novels by Allan N. Packer at *Amazon's Kindle Store* and other major online bookstores.

ACKNOWLEDGMENTS

Special thanks to my beta readers, Merilyn, Deborah, and Ray. They offered useful feedback and suggestions for improvements.

My thanks to Karri, who came up with a great cover as always.

My grateful thanks go to Brian Plush for the awesome map.

Finally, thanks go to God, the source of creativity.

ABOUT THE AUTHOR

Allan Packer is an emerging author of epic fantasy. *The Rending* is his first novelette, following his novels *The Stone of Knowing* and *The Cost of Knowing*.

Allan grew up surrounded by books and became an avid reader during his childhood. In his university years fantasy displaced science fiction as his favorite genre, thanks primarily to J. R. R. Tolkien. He later shared this love with his four children by reading The Lord of the Rings to them aloud—a three-month marathon he completed twice during their formative years.

Born in Australia, Allan has lived and worked on three continents, and spent one quarter of his working years abroad. Having worked as an IT professional throughout his career, he was first published as a technical author.

Today he lives with his wife in Adelaide, South Australia, near their children and a small but growing band of grandchildren.

Allan is currently working on the next installment in his series *The Stone Cycle*.